The Perfectly imperfect boyfriend

Art Vulcan

Published by Art Vulcan, 2024.

This is a work of fiction. Similarities to real people, places, or events are entirely coincidental.

THE PERFECTLY IMPERFECT BOYFRIEND

First edition. October 6, 2024.

Copyright © 2024 Art Vulcan.

ISBN: 979-8227949141

Written by Art Vulcan.

Table of Contents

Chapter 1: 1
Chapter 2: 6
Chapter 3: 10
Chapter 5: 14
Chapter 6: 17
Chapter 7: 20
Chapter 8: 23
Chapter 9: 26
Chapter 10: 30
Chapter 11: 33
Chapter 12: 36
Chapter 13: 40
Chapter 14: 42
Chapter 15: 45
Chapter 16: 47
Chapter 17: 50
Chapter 18: 53

Chapter 1:

The sun beat down on Laura's back as she rummaged through the cluttered garage sale, her eyes searching for a treasure amidst the forgotten junk. She'd been looking for something unique to spruce up her room, something that could make her forget about school and the mundane routines that filled her days. Her fingertips grazed over dusty action figures and chipped ceramic mugs until they reached something cool and smooth.

It was a lamp, unlike any she'd ever seen. Its intricate brass design looked as if it had been plucked from the pages of a storybook, and she couldn't resist the urge to pick it up. Laura turned it over in her hands, admiring the way the metal gleamed even under the harsh sun. It felt heavier than she'd expected, almost like it contained a secret. Without much thought, she rubbed the lamp with the sleeve of her shirt, and suddenly, the world around her seemed to hold its breath.

A puff of smoke shot out from the lamp's spout, and within seconds, it grew into a thick, swirling cloud. Laura's heart raced as she stumbled back, dropping the lamp. The cloud began to coalesce into a human form, and she watched in disbelief as a man appeared before her, dressed in a flashy, silken outfit that was a dizzying mix of colors. He had a beard that curled at the ends and a mischievous twinkle in his eye that made her simultaneously curious and wary.

"Young lady," the genie said, bowing with a flourish, "you have freed me from my eternal prison, and for that, I am eternally grateful. In return, I shall grant you three wishes." His voice was like smooth velvet, and Laura felt a thrill run through her as she realized this wasn't a hallucination or some kind of prank. This was real.

Her mind raced, trying to come up with the perfect wish. A new car? A trip to Paris? But as she gazed into the genie's ancient eyes, she knew she had to be careful. "What's the catch?" she asked, her skepticism tempering her excitement.

The genie chuckled, a sound that echoed through the stillness of the garage sale. "Ah, young one," he said, "there is always a catch. But fear not, for I am bound by the laws of the wish-granter. Your wishes must be clear, and I shall not deceive you with trickery or malicious intent. However, beware the unforeseen consequences that may arise from hasty desires."

Laura took a deep breath, trying to steady her nerves. "Okay," she said, her voice trembling slightly. "For my first wish, I wish for the perfect boyfriend." It was a wish she'd harbored since she first picked up a romance novel, a candy-coated dream of love and happiness.

The genie's expression grew serious. "Very well," he said, raising a finger. "Your wish is granted."

With that, the world around Laura seemed to blur for a moment, and when it snapped back into focus, there he was—Logan. A tall, handsome figure emerged from the garage sale's shadows, his eyes locking onto hers as if he'd been searching for her all his life. He was utterly flawless, with a chiseled jaw, piercing blue eyes, and a cascade of chestnut hair that seemed to defy gravity. Laura's breath hitched in her chest as he approached, moving with the grace of someone who knew exactly how to make an entrance.

"Hey, Laura," he said, flashing a smile so brilliant it could have lit up the garage on its own. "It's a pretty hot day, isn't it?" His voice was a perfect blend of warmth and charm, and she felt her cheeks flush as she nodded.

Logan looked around, taking in the chaos of the garage sale with a bemused expression. "You know," he said, "I've always had a soft spot for these kinds of places. You never know what kind of treasure you might find." His eyes met hers again, and Laura felt as though she was drowning in their depths.

He was everything she'd ever wanted in a boyfriend. He held the door open for her when they left the garage, and on their first date, he took her to her favorite restaurant—a cozy Italian place downtown that she'd mentioned once in passing. He ordered her usual without asking and had a bouquet of her favorite flowers—wildflowers—waiting for her at the table. The way he listened to her, really listened, made Laura feel like she was the most interesting person in the world.

They talked for hours, their laughter echoing through the dimly lit dining room. Logan told her about his love for reading, which coincidentally matched her own, and his passion for cooking. He was a star soccer player, which was convenient because Laura was the team's biggest fan. And when he held her hand, it felt like she'd known him forever, like the universe had finally clicked into place.

The whispers at school grew louder as their relationship bloomed. Girls shot her envious glances, and boys nudged each other, muttering about what a lucky break Laura had stumbled upon. The couple became the talk of the town, and she basked in the warmth of his attention, his every gesture calculated to make her heart flutter.

"So, Laura," he said one day as they strolled through the park, "what's your favorite book?"

"Oh, that's easy," Laura replied with a smile. "It's 'Pride and Prejudice.' I love the wit and the romance."

Logan's eyes lit up. "I've read that one. Mr. Darcy's quite the catch, isn't he?" He leaned closer, whispering conspiratorially, "But I've always had a soft spot for Lizzie Bennet."

Laura laughed, feeling a spark of genuine connection. "Yeah, she's pretty amazing," she said, her voice a little breathless. "So smart and witty."

"Absolutely," Logan agreed, his eyes never leaving hers. "Someone who knows their own worth, that's what I admire." He squeezed her hand, and Laura felt a thrill at the touch.

As the days turned into weeks, Laura found herself lost in the whirlwind of her newfound romance. Logan was attentive, bringing her little gifts like chocolates and hand-picked flowers for no reason at all. He'd show up at her games, cheering her on from the stands, and surprise her with picnics under the stars. The whispers grew to a crescendo as their relationship grew stronger, and Laura basked in the attention.

"Hey, Laura," her classmate Rachel said one day at lunch, her eyes narrowing as she watched Logan from across the cafeteria. "How did you manage to snag him? He's like, the holy grail of boyfriends."

Laura felt a twinge of pride mixed with a hint of unease. "I don't know," she replied with a shrug, trying to play it cool. "We just clicked, I guess."

Rachel rolled her eyes. "Please, Laura. Spill it. You can't just stumble upon a guy like that. There's gotta be a secret."

"I wish there was," Laura said with a laugh, feeling the warmth of a blush spread across her cheeks. "But it's all just good timing, I guess."

Rachel leaned in closer, her curiosity piqued. "Well, if you ever do figure it out, you've got to tell me," she whispered, her voice a mix of awe and envy. Laura nodded, unable to tear her gaze away from Logan as he approached.

"Hey, Rach," Logan said, giving Rachel a charming smile. "How's your day going?" Rachel's cheeks turned a shade of red that Laura had never seen before, and she babbled an incoherent response before scurrying away. Laura couldn't help but feel a thrill of satisfaction at Rachel's reaction. It was like having a celebrity for a boyfriend, and everyone knew it.

Chapter 2:

The whispers grew louder, and the glances more frequent as the weeks passed. Laura found herself floating through school on a cloud of happiness, her every move scrutinized and envied by her peers. The feeling was addictive, and she reveled in it, sharing sweet kisses with Logan in the hallways and holding his hand as they walked to class.

"What's the secret, Laura?" her friends would ask, their eyes wide with wonder. "How do you keep him so in love with you?" Laura just smiled and shrugged, feeling a thrill at the mystery she'd become. It was as if she'd been granted a fairytale, and everyone wanted the spellbook.

But as the initial excitement of her wish-made romance began to wane, Laura couldn't shake the feeling that something was off. Logan was perfect, almost too perfect. He never forgot an anniversary, never had a bad hair day, and always knew exactly what to say to make her smile. The spontaneity of a real relationship seemed to elude them. Every kiss felt rehearsed, every conversation a script they'd recited a hundred times before.

One evening, as they sat together on the couch watching her favorite movie—which just so happened to be Logan's favorite too—Laura glanced over and saw that his eyes weren't even on the screen. They were fixed on her, studying her every reaction, waiting for the cue to laugh or to lean in for a kiss. It was like he was a puppet, and she was pulling the strings. The realization hit her like a ton of bricks.

"Logan," she said, pausing the movie, "are you okay?"

He blinked, looking surprised by the interruption. "Oh, yes," he said, his smile never faltering. "Why do you ask?"

"It's just..." Laura struggled to find the right words. "You're always so... perfect. You never disagree with me, you never get upset. It's like you're not even real."

Logan's smile slipped for the briefest of moments before reassembling itself. "I'm here to make you happy," he said, his voice still velvety. "Isn't that what you wanted?"

But Laura couldn't shake the feeling that there was something wrong with this picture. "I don't know," she admitted. "Maybe I just miss the little things. Like when guys forget your favorite color or when they accidentally spill soda on the couch. It's like we don't have any real moments together."

Logan nodded, his expression thoughtful. "I understand," he said, his eyes never leaving hers. "But remember, I'm here for you, Laura. To give you what you want."

The words hung in the air, and Laura felt a coldness creep into her heart. Was that all he was? A means to an end, a living, breathing manifestation of her desires? It was as if she'd created a boyfriend in a lab, one that was perfect on paper but lacked the messy, unpredictable spark of life.

As the days went on, Laura found herself longing for the imperfections she used to scoff at in the boys she'd known before Logan. The way they'd trip over their own feet, their laugh that was more of a snort, the occasional bad mood that made them seem more human. With Logan, there was never any of that.

Meanwhile, unbeknownst to her, Jake, the boy next door, had been watching from the sidelines. He'd seen Laura's transformation from a girl who loved adventure and spontaneity to one who was caught in the grips of a fairytale that felt more like a prison. His heart ached as he watched her laugh at Logan's rehearsed jokes and share stories that had lost their luster in the face of perfection. They'd been best friends since they were kids, sharing scraped knees and secret handshakes. But now, it was like she was in a different world, one that didn't have room for him.

Jake had always had feelings for Laura, but he'd never had the courage to tell her. He'd watched her date guys who were wrong for her, hoping each one would be the wake-up call she needed to see what was right in front of her. But Logan was different. He was everything Laura had ever said she wanted, and it was killing Jake to see her with someone who didn't know her the way he did. He knew the real Laura, the one who liked to stay up all night talking about their dreams and fears, the one who'd eat a whole pizza and still be hungry for more.

He'd observed her from afar since the day she'd wished for the perfect boyfriend. He'd seen the way she'd light up when Logan walked into the room, the way she'd laugh at his jokes even when they weren't funny, and the way she'd follow him like a lost puppy. It was as if she'd forgotten who she was, forgotten the adventures they'd had together, climbing trees and racing bikes until the sun went down. Jake had never felt so powerless, so he did the only thing he could think of: he waited, hoping she'd realize that perfection was overrated.

But as the months went by, Laura grew more distant. The spontaneous bike rides and late-night chats were replaced by carefully coordinated dates and public displays of affection that seemed more for show than for their hearts. Rachel and the other girls at school whispered about Laura's fairytale romance, but Jake could see the cracks beneath the surface. The way Laura's eyes would sometimes glaze over when Logan talked about his latest soccer victory, the way she'd sigh when he suggested they watch the same movie for the fifth time that week.

Jake tried to keep their friendship alive, inviting her over to hang out or to grab ice cream, but Logan was always there, a constant presence that seemed to suck the air out of the room. Laura was different with him around, her laughs forced and her smiles never quite reaching her eyes. It was like watching a shadow of his best friend, and it was breaking Jake's heart.

He'd always loved Laura, but he'd never had the guts to tell her. Now, with Logan in the picture, it felt like his chance had passed. He'd sit on the porch swing, watching them walk hand in hand down the street, and he'd wonder what it would be like to be the one making her happy.

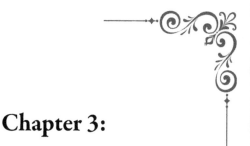

Chapter 3:

One afternoon, as Laura sat on her front lawn, lost in thought, Jake mustered the courage to join her. He'd noticed a sadness in her eyes that Logan's perfection couldn't mask, and he couldn't stand by anymore. "Hey, Laura," he called out, his voice tentative.

She looked up, surprised, as he settled next to her on the grass. They hadn't had a real conversation in weeks. "Hey, Jake," she said, a small smile playing on her lips. "What's up?"

Jake took a deep breath, his heart racing. "I just wanted to check on you," he said, trying to sound casual. "You've been kind of... different lately."

Laura looked at him, a flicker of something—was it sadness or annoyance?—flitting across her face. "Different?"

Jake nodded, plucking at a piece of grass. "Yeah. You know, like... not you."

Laura's eyes searched his, and for the first time in what felt like forever, she saw something genuine, something that cut through the glossy façade of her new life. "What do you mean?"

Jake took a deep breath. "You used to laugh at the dumbest stuff," he said, a fond smile tugging at the corners of his lips. "And now, every time you laugh, it seems like you're trying too hard."

Laura felt a pang of guilt, her heart squeezing in her chest. It was true; she'd been living in a bubble of perfection, afraid to let the air out for fear of what might happen. She'd been so focused on the idea of a perfect relationship that she'd forgotten what it felt like to be herself, to argue and make up and learn from her mistakes. With Logan, there was never any room for growth, no opportunity to navigate the rocky terrain of real love. It was all smooth sailing, and she was starting to feel like she was drowning in the calm waters.

As the leaves began to change, Laura found herself craving the storms that used to sweep through her life, the kind that brought growth and change. She missed the unpredictability, the way a simple "I don't know" from a boy could send her heart racing with the thrill of the unknown. But with Logan, she always knew. He was like a well-rehearsed play, hitting every cue without fail.

One evening, as they sat side by side on her bed, flipping through a photo album of their seemingly perfect moments, Laura's finger hovered over a picture of her and Jake, taken during their treehouse building escapade the summer before. A real laugh bubbled up, one that had been buried beneath layers of forced giggles. Logan looked at her, a puzzled expression on his flawless face. "What's funny?" he asked.

Laura sighed, setting the album aside. "It's just that Jake and I used to argue all the time," she said, her voice wistful. "But we'd always make up and do something stupid together."

Logan's smile never wavered. "Ah, yes," he said. "The thrill of the chase."

But Laura knew that wasn't it. The chase was fun, but it was the journey that made it worthwhile. With Logan, there was no journey, just a destination she'd arrived at without ever leaving the starting line.

So, Laura hatched a plan. If she couldn't get him to mess up naturally, she'd force it. First stop: an all-you-can-eat buffet, where she hoped food coma would loosen his perfection's grip. She watched with glee as he piled his plate with pizza, pasta, and nachos—foods she'd never seen him touch before. But even as he ate, he remained poised, not a crumb daring to cling to his pristine shirt. Laura tried to trip him up with spicy salsa and cheesy strings that stretched between his mouth and plate, but he handled them with the grace of a seasoned food critic. She laughed, but it was a hollow sound.

Next, she dragged him to the school dance, throwing him into a spontaneous dance-off with her friends. Logan, who'd never shown an interest in dancing, took the challenge with the ease of a seasoned pro. He twirled her around, dipped her dramatically, and even bust out some breakdance moves that had the whole school's jaws dropping. Laura felt like a prop in his perfect performance, and her frustration grew.

"Come on, Logan, mess up just once!" she whispered to him, her voice desperate. But his eyes just sparkled with mischief. "Why would I do that, darling?" he replied, spinning her again.

The dance floor was a blur of color and movement, but Laura's focus remained solely on her genie-given boyfriend. She'd hoped that maybe, just maybe, in the chaos of the school dance, she'd catch a glimpse of the boy who didn't always know the right moves, the boy who might get a little clumsy or sweaty. But no. Logan's rhythm was impeccable, his smile never faltered, and his hair remained perfectly in place, not a single strand daring to move out of its meticulously styled pattern.

"This is ridiculous," Laura murmured to herself, her feet aching in her too-tight shoes. "Even when I try to trip him up, he's flawless."

"You okay?" Logan leaned in, his breath minty fresh despite the mountain of garlic bread he'd just devoured. "You seem a bit... tense."

"I'm fine," Laura said through gritted teeth. "Just peachy." She scanned the crowded dance floor for a way out of this nightmare. "Why don't we go grab some punch?"

"But the dance-off isn't over yet," Logan said, his smile not missing a beat as he spun her into another twirl.

Laura felt her patience wearing thinner than the soles of her dancing shoes. "Okay, okay," he said, his voice charming as ever. "Let's take a break."

They made their way through the crowd to the punch bowl, where she filled two cups to the brim, hoping that maybe, just maybe, she could get him to spill it on his shirt. But as they sipped their drinks, his movements remained as graceful as ever.

"This is ridiculous," Laura muttered under her breath.

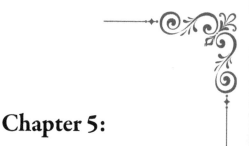

Chapter 5:

Laura continues her attempts to shake Logan's perfection by "forgetting" their three-month anniversary. She avoids the topic, hoping he'd get upset or at least show some sign of human emotion. But when the day passes without even a hint of annoyance from him, Laura can't help but feel a twinge of disappointment.

"Logan," she says, her voice tight with frustration, "I totally forgot about our anniversary today."

Logan's smile doesn't falter. " Laura, it's no big deal," he says, stroking her cheek gently. "I know you've had a lot on your plate lately."

Laura's jaw clenches. "But it's our three-month anniversary!" she exclaims. "How could you not be upset?"

Logan chuckles, his eyes sparkling. "Why should I be upset, my dear?" he asks, his voice smooth as silk. "You're more than enough of a present for me every day."

Laura's eyes narrow. "Seriously?" she says, her voice laced with skepticism. "You're not even a little bit mad?"

"Why would I be mad, Laura?" Logan's smile is so bright it could have powered the school's lights. "Our love isn't measured in days or gifts. It's something much more profound."

THE PERFECTLY IMPERFECT BOYFRIEND 15

Laura's eyes searched his, looking for a crack in the armor. "But everyone gets mad," she insists. "It's normal."

Logan's hand rests on her shoulder, his touch feather-light. "Not everyone is like everyone else," he counters. "I'm here to make you happy, Laura. And seeing you upset over something so trivial as an anniversary? That doesn't make me happy."

Laura sighs, flopping onto her bed and tossing her phone aside. It's been a long day of forced laughter and fake smiles, and she just can't take it anymore. She picks up her pillow and hugs it tightly to her chest, wishing she could just scream into it and let all her frustrations out. But she knows that won't solve anything. She needs to talk to someone who gets it, someone who's known her since she was knee-high to a grasshopper.

Her eyes drift to the window, and she sees Jake's light on in the house next door. Before she can overthink it, she's slipped into her flip-flops and is crossing the dew-dampened lawn. She taps lightly on his window, and a moment later, it opens with a soft creak.

"Hey, Laura," Jake whispers, his voice thick with sleep. "What's up?"

Laura climbs through the window, her eyes brimming with tears. "I can't do it anymore," she says, collapsing onto his bed. "Logan's perfect, but he's not... real."

Jake's eyes widen, and he sits up, pushing his messy hair out of his face. "What do you mean?" he asks, his voice hushed.

Laura takes a deep breath, the weight of her secret pressing on her chest. "Remember that lamp I bought at the garage sale?" she starts. "Well, it turns out there was a genie inside."

Jake blinks, rubbing sleep from his eyes. "A genie? Like, a real one?"

"Yeah," Laura says with a sigh. "I know it sounds crazy, but he was right there, all smoke and lights and... and... he granted me three wishes."

Jake stares at her, his mind racing. "And one of those wishes was for Logan?"

Laura nods, her eyes glistening with unshed tears. "Yeah. I wanted the perfect boyfriend, and I got him. But now, I realize that perfection is... it's not what I thought it would be."

Jake sits there, stunned. "So, you mean to say that Logan isn't real?"

Laura wipes at her eyes with the back of her hand. "Well, he's real, but he's not... human," she explains. " I.. I don't know what he is, it's complicated, I wished him into existence."

Jake is silent for a moment, taking this in. "Wow," he says finally, his voice filled with a mix of disbelief and something else Laura can't quite identify. "That's... heavy."

"You don't know the half of it," Laura says, her voice shaking. "Everything he does is perfect, every word, every gesture. But it's like... it's not real. It's like I'm dating a robot."

Jake nods, his expression a mix of confusion and concern. "So, what are you going to do?"

Laura shrugs, her shoulders heavy with the weight of her decision. "I don't know," she admits.

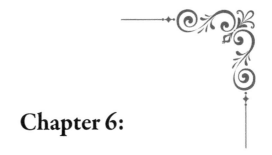

Chapter 6:

Jake swallows hard, his heart racing in his chest. This was it, the moment he'd been waiting for, the moment he'd feared. He reaches over, taking Laura's hand in his. "I need to tell you something," he says, his voice barely above a whisper.

Laura looks up at him, her eyes red from crying. "What is it?" she asks, her voice small.

Jake takes a deep breath, feeling his heart hammer in his chest. "I've been in love with you since forever," he says, his voice cracking a little. "But when Logan showed up, I didn't want to mess up what you had. I thought if I waited long enough, you'd see that he wasn't what you needed."

Laura's eyes widen, her grip on the pillow tightening. She'd never expected to hear those words from Jake, not when she was in the throes of a supposedly perfect relationship. But as she looks into his eyes, she sees the truth in them, the raw emotion that Logan's flawless exterior could never match.

Her mind reels with the implications of Jake's confession. She'd always felt comfortable with him, safe, like she could be her true self. But love? She'd never thought about it, not like this. It was as if a door she'd never noticed before had suddenly been thrown open, revealing a room filled with memories of shared laughter and stolen glances.

For a moment, Laura is silent, processing this revelation. Then, she whispers, "Jake, I had no idea."

Jake nods, his eyes never leaving hers. "I know it's a lot," he says softly.

Laura feels a lump form in her throat, the weight of his words pressing down on her. "But why didn't you tell me?" she asks, her voice barely above a whisper.

Jake sighs, his gaze dropping to their intertwined hands. "I thought you were happy and I was scared," he says, his voice thick with emotion. "I didn't want to be the one to mess it up."

Laura's heart skips a beat. She'd been so focused on the ideal that she'd missed the real. Jake's confession echoes through her like a bell, resonating with the quiet truth she'd been too afraid to admit. She thinks back to all the moments they'd shared, the countless hours of laughter and tears, the secret handshakes that no one else knew. With Logan, she had perfection, but with Jake, she had history.

Her eyes search Jake's face, finding a warmth that Logan's perfect smile could never match. In the quiet of his room, with the faint smell of old baseball gloves and fresh-cut grass, Laura feels like she's come home. The realization hits her like a wave: she's been so busy chasing a fantasy that she'd forgotten the comfort of the familiar.

But Jake's words hang in the air, a confession that could shake the very foundation of her world.

she'd spent a ton of money for a designer wardrobe, thinking it would somehow make her feel more worthy of her perfect boyfriend. She'd wanted to be arm-candy, a flawless accessory to his perfection. The irony isn't lost on her; she'd been so focused on the exterior that she'd forgotten the importance of what was inside.

When she opens her eyes, she sees Jake's hopeful gaze, the same one that had been there for her through every scraped knee and failed test. He'd been her constant, her north star in a world of ever-changing tides. And now, as she sits here in his room, she wonders how she could have ever thought perfection was what she needed.

The silence stretches between them, filled with the quiet hum of a thousand unspoken words. Laura's mind is a whirlwind of emotions, torn between the safety of the known and the allure of the unexplored. She thinks of Logan, of his perfect dates and the way he says all the right things, and she feels a pang of sadness. Because as perfect as he was, he could never replace the history she had with Jake, the shared jokes that only they found funny, the way his laughter had always made her feel like she could conquer the world.

Looking into Jake's eyes, Laura sees a reflection of herself that she's missed: the girl who used to climb trees and eat ice cream cones in the rain, who didn't need a boyfriend to validate her existence. She feels the warmth of his hand around hers and realizes that maybe, just maybe, she's been chasing the wrong kind of fairy tale.

Chapter 7:

Laura's thoughts are racing, Laura pulls her hand away, her mind made up. She has to tell Logan the truth. She can't keep living this lie anymore. She can't keep pretending that a scripted relationship is what she wants. So she takes a deep breath and says the words she's been rehearsing all night. "Logan, I need to tell you something."

His smile falters, just for a moment, before it's back in place. "Of course, Laura," he says, his voice soothing. "What is it?"

Laura's heart pounds in her chest as she gathers her courage. "Logan," she starts, her voice trembling. "I... I think I made a mistake."

He looks at her, his expression unreadable. "A mistake?" he echoes. "What could you possibly mean?"

Laura gathers her resolve. "I wish for you to never have existed," she says, the words tasting like ash in her mouth. She'd thought it would be a simple solution, a way to undo the genie's work and start fresh. But as she speaks, she feels a strange heaviness settle over her.

The genie, floating in the corner of the room, shakes its head. "I'm afraid it's not that simple, Laura," it says, its voice echoing with an ancient sadness. "Once a being has been brought to life, they cannot be simply 'unwished' away."

THE PERFECTLY IMPERFECT BOYFRIEND 21

Laura's eyes widen with horror. "What are you saying?" she whispers. "I can't just make him disappear?"

The genie sighs, its smoke form rippling with an unspoken understanding. "Your wish has created a paradox," it explains. "Logan is not merely a construct of your desires but a living, sentient being with his own essence."

Laura feels a chill run down her spine. "What are you saying?" she whispers, her eyes wide with horror.

"It's not something you can just wish away. Logan is a real person now, with his own thoughts, feelings, and life." The genie says solemnly, its eyes meeting Laura's with a gravity she's never seen before. "Magic cannot unmake life once it's been granted. If you wish to be rid of him, you must do so in the traditional way."

Laura's stomach twists into a knot. "You mean... I have to... kill him?" she stammers, the words feeling foreign and heavy on her tongue.

The genie nods solemnly. "It is the only way to release him from the confines of your wish," it explains. "To wish for his non-existence is to wish for the end of his life."

Laura feels sick, the color draining from her face. She never meant for it to go this far. She just wanted to feel something real again, not this plastic, picture-perfect romance.

"But he's not human," she argues weakly. "He's... he's a wish."

The genie's eyes bore into hers, unblinking. "Wish or not, once given life, the soul cannot be un-lived," it says firmly. Laura's thoughts swirl with the gravity of the situation. It wasn't like she was going to kill a human being—Logan had never truly existed before she'd wished him into being. But the thought of erasing someone from the fabric of reality was a weight she wasn't sure she could bear.

Her mind races back to the day she'd made that flippant wish. How could she have been so naive? She'd wanted a fairy tale without realizing that even in fairy tales, there's always a catch. And now, here she was, faced with the harsh reality of her own creation.

The room feels suffocating, the walls closing in as Laura grapples with the gravity of her decision. The genie's words echo in her mind, leaving her with a heavy heart. She thinks back to the carefree days before the lamp, the days when she didn't know perfection could be so stifling. She remembers Jake's comforting presence, his genuine smile that didn't need to be wished into existence. Laura knew what she had to do; she had to free herself from the shackles of her own creation.

But as she turns to face the genie, she's stopped by the sound of footsteps outside her bedroom door. Logan bursts in, his face a mask of rage and fear—emotions Laura had never seen on his perfect features. "You can't do this to me," he says, his voice shaking. "I know what you're planning."

Chapter 8:

Laura's eyes widen, her heart racing. "Logan, I..." she starts, but he cuts her off.

"How could you?" he demands, his voice trembling with a rawness that Laura had never heard before. "You created me to be perfect, to make you happy, and now you want to throw it all away?"

Laura's eyes fill with tears as she looks at the boy she thought she knew so well. "I didn't know," she whispers, her voice barely above a breath. "I didn't know you'd be real, that you'd have feelings."

Logan's eyes are wide, his perfect facade shattering before her very eyes. "I thought you loved me," he says, his voice cracking. "I did everything for you."

Laura feels a pang of guilt, looking at the desperation etched into his features. But she knows she can't keep living a lie. "Logan," she says, her voice shaking. "I don't know what to do."

Logan's eyes search hers, a storm of emotions swirling in their depths. "You don't love me," he says, his voice cracking. "You never did. I was just a means to an end."

Laura's heart aches at the pain in his voice, a pain she never knew a perfect being could feel. She takes a step towards him, her hand reaching out tentatively. "Logan," she says softly. "It's not like that. I just... I need something real."

But Logan isn't listening, his eyes wild with a fear that Laura never knew could exist in his flawless features. "I'm real!" he insists, his voice rising. "I have feelings, I have a heart!" He places a hand over his chest, as if to prove his point. Laura watches him, feeling the weight of his panic like a stone in her stomach.

With a roar of anger and despair, Logan storms out of the room, slamming the door so hard the pictures on the wall rattle. Laura hears his footsteps pound down the stairs, the front door fly open, and then the sound of his retreating footsteps fade into the night.

Her mind races as she looks at the genie, who still floats calmly in the corner. "What have I done?" she asks, her voice shaking.

The genie regards her solemnly. "You've learned a valuable lesson, Laura," it says. "Perfection is a fleeting and unattainable ideal. What truly matters is the love that comes from imperfection."

The genie vanished leaving Laura alone with her thoughts, With a heavy heart, Laura nods. "I need to fix this," she says, her voice determined. She jumps into action, her mind racing with ideas. Maybe there's a way to make things right without hurting Logan.

Her first stop is a quirky little fortune teller's tent at the local carnival. The woman inside, a plump lady with a crystal ball the size of a watermelon, listens to Laura's story with a knowing smile. "Ah, the curse of perfection," she says, her voice lilting with a Eastern European accent. "Very common mistake for those who wish without thought."

THE PERFECTLY IMPERFECT BOYFRIEND

Laura nods eagerly. "Please, do you know any way to reverse it?"

The fortune teller's smile widens. "It is a powerful force, but also a fickle one. You cannot simply wish away the heart's true desires."

Laura's eyes plead with her. "But he's not real!" she insists. "I made him up!"

The fortune teller's smile doesn't waver. "Real or not, love is a powerful force," she says. "You gave him life with your wish, and now you must deal with the consequences."

Feeling desperate, Laura decides to give it a shot. She leaves the tent with a sprig of lavender and a cryptic incantation scribbled on a napkin. She heads home, her mind racing with the absurdity of the situation. How did she end up in a world where she had to perform spells to fix a relationship she'd wished into existence? She laughs to herself, the sound a little too high-pitched.

Chapter 9:

Laura's first attempt at amateur spellcasting is a disaster. The ingredients she finds in her kitchen—flour, eggs, and a dash of hope—create a concoction that looks more like a failed soufflé than a love potion. The smoke alarm shrieks, and Laura waves a dish towel around the room, coughing as the mess congeals on the stove.

Undeterred, Laura tries convincing the genie to break its own rules. She finds him lounging on her living room couch, watching reality TV. "Come on," she begs. "You've gotta have some kind of loophole. Can't you just poof him back into the lamp?"

The genie looks at her over the rim of his sunglasses, not even bothering to pause the show. "Rules are rules," he says, his tone as dry as the desert he'd been trapped in for centuries. "And love potions are so passé."

Laura throws up her hands in frustration, the napkin with the incantation fluttering to the floor. "But he's not even human!" she exclaims. "What if he hurts someone?"

The genie sighs, flicking the TV off with a snap of his fingers. "As much as I'd love to help, I can't," he says.

"But why not?" Laura asks, her voice desperate.

The genie shakes its head. "Because love is not something that can be wished away or rewritten," it explains. "It's a force of nature, as wild and unpredictable as a tornado. And you, my dear, have stirred up a storm."

With the genie's words echoing in her ears, Laura turns to her bookshelf, searching for any book that might hold the key to undoing her wish. Her eyes land on a dusty, leather-bound tome titled "The Art of Spellcasting." With trembling hands, she opens it and starts to read. The incantations within are complex, with ingredients she's never heard of before. But she's desperate, and so she gathers her courage and begins to experiment.

Her first attempt is a mess. Laura mixes eye of newt and wing of bat, whispering ancient words under her breath. Her living room fills with a thick, purple smoke, and she ends up sneezing more than casting a spell but Laura's not one to give up easily. She clears the air and tries again, her eyes focused on the page, her voice steady.

Logan, on the other hand, is in full-blown survival mode. He's Googling "How to prove you're real to a girl who wishes you weren't." He even goes as far as hiring a lawyer—a very confused one at that—to draft a legal contract stating his existence. He starts to study philosophy, hoping to find some profound argument to sway Laura's heart.

In the school library, Logan is surrounded by dusty tomes and the smell of old ink, his brow furrowed as he pores over existential texts. He's lost in thought, scribbling notes on a legal pad as he tries to find a logical argument to convince Laura that he's more than just a wish-born facade. Jake walks by, raising an eyebrow at the sight of the school's golden boy in such a state of intellectual distress.

"What's up, Romeo?" he asks, smirking.

Logan looks up from his pile of books, his eyes red-rimmed and desperate. "It's Laura," he says, his voice tight. "I think she's going to try to get rid of me."

Jake's smirk fades, and he crosses his arms over his chest. "And why would she do that?"

Logan's eyes are pleading. "Because she thinks I'm not real," he says, his voice cracking. "Because she thinks I'm just a... a thing she created."

Jake's face falls, his heart aching for the friend who's been caught in Laura's fairy tale gone wrong. "You are real," he says firmly. "You're a person, with feelings and thoughts and... and a really annoying way of always being perfect."

Logan gives a watery smile, appreciating the attempt at humor. "Thanks," he says, his voice a little stronger. "But she doesn't see it that way. She thinks I'm just a... a puppet she wished into being."

Jake's heart squeezes. He knows he can't just stand by while Laura tries to erase Logan. He has to do something, anything to help his friend.

"Okay," Jake says slowly, his mind racing. "I'll help you."

Logan's head snaps up, hope lighting his eyes. "What? Really?"

Jake nods solemnly. "As much as I love Laura, I can't just let her do this," he says, his voice firm. "You're not just a thing to me."

Logan's eyes well up with gratitude, and the two of them share a moment of understanding that feels strange and yet oddly right. Despite their history, despite their feelings for Laura, they are now bound by a shared goal: to preserve Logan's existence.

Together, they hatch a plan to outsmart Laura. They know her well, her quirks and her habits, her tendency to go all out when she's determined. They anticipate her moves, setting up decoys and distractions, turning her own perfectionism against her.

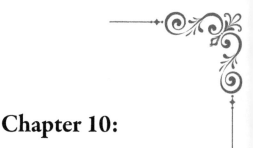

Chapter 10:

One day, Laura comes home to find a bouquet of flowers that somehow seem more perfect than any she's ever seen before. She knows immediately it's Logan's doing, a last-ditch effort to win her back. But as she reaches for the bouquet, it transforms into a cloud of glitter that fills the room, blinding her. She stumbles, coughing, as Jake and Logan emerge from behind the curtain, grinning like conspirators.

"What the hell?" Laura sputters, her eyes watering.

Jake steps forward, his expression apologetic. "Look, Laura, I know you're confused and you think you made a mistake, but you can't just get rid of someone because they're not what you thought you wanted."

Laura's eyes narrow, the frustration boiling over. "You don't understand," she says through gritted teeth. "This isn't real. It's not fair to any of us."

But Jake's expression is firm. "Maybe not," he admits. "But you can't just wish him away."

Laura's hand hovers over the glitter, her mind racing. She looks at Logan, who's staring at her with a mix of hope and fear. And for the first time, she sees the cracks in his perfection. His usually immaculate hair is a little messy, his smile not quite as bright as she's used to.

"What's happening to you?" she asks, her voice filled with a mix of wonder and concern.

Logan runs a hand through his hair, which, to Laura's shock, is not perfectly styled. "I don't know," he says, his voice trembling. "Ever since you... ever since you said you didn't want me to exist..."

He looks down at his hands, which are trembling slightly. Laura notices for the first time that he has a smudge of dirt on his cheek, and his shirt is not tucked in just so. "I've been feeling... different," he confesses.

Laura's eyes widen as she watches him. She's never seen Logan anything less than perfect. But here he is, fumbling with his words, his movements awkward and uncertain. And it's strange, but she feels something stir inside her chest—a warmth that wasn't there before. "How?" she asks, her voice gentle.

Logan shrugs, looking at her with a sad smile. "I think... I think it's because you don't love me," he says. "The perfect boyfriend doesn't exist anymore."

Laura's eyes widen as she takes in his slightly rumpled appearance. She's never seen him like this before. He looks... human. "What do you mean?" she asks, her voice tentative.

Logan sighs, the sound heavy with a sadness she's never heard from him. "Every time you look at me with doubt, every time you question whether I'm real." he says. "I can feel myself becoming... less than perfect."

Laura's eyes widen as she takes in his slightly rumpled appearance. He's never been anything less than impeccable before. His shirt is untucked, his hair has a mind of its own, and his eyes... there's a vulnerability in them that she's never noticed.

The next few days, Laura watches Logan stumble through life, making mistake after mistake. He spills coffee on himself, forgets her favorite movie, and even burns the dinner he'd meticulously prepared to win her back. His jokes are corny, and he trips over his own feet. But instead of the irritation she'd felt before, Laura feels a strange fondness.

One afternoon, while they're walking in the park, Logan tries to show off his "cool moves" on a skateboard—a hobby Laura had told him she liked. He wipes out spectacularly, landing on his backside with a thump. Laura can't help but laugh as she helps him up, brushing the dust from his jeans. His cheeks redden, and he shoots her a sheepish grin that makes her heart stutter. "Not so perfect now, huh?" he says, his voice filled with self-deprecation.

Their dates become less about grand gestures and more about simple moments of shared laughter and connection. Laura finds herself smiling more, relaxing in his company. The way he stumbles over his words when he's nervous, the way his eyes crinkle when he laughs, the way he chews on his bottom lip when he's concentrating—these are the things that make him real to her.

Chapter 11:

One evening, as Laura and Logan sit on her bedroom floor eating burnt popcorn and watching a terrible movie, Laura looks over at him and feels something she's never felt before—genuine affection. "You know, you're not so bad," she says, smiling.

Logan laughs, his eyes shimmering with relief. "Thanks," he says, his voice light. "I've been trying to tell you that."

They sit in companionable silence for a while, the TV playing in the background, the smell of burnt popcorn lingering in the air. Laura can't help but feel a warmth towards him that she's never felt before. It's strange, but the more imperfect he becomes, the more she finds herself caring for him. The genie's words come back to her: "What truly matters is the love that comes from imperfection." Maybe, she thinks, it's not about finding the perfect boyfriend, but about learning to love someone for who they are, flaws and all.

The question now is, can she let go of her need for control and accept that she might have gotten more than she bargained for? Can she look past the fact that he was a wish and see the person he's become? Laura chews on her bottom lip, her mind racing with the implications of her decision. If she goes through with the spell to erase him, she's not just letting go of a perfect fantasy—she's ending the life of someone who's grown to mean something to her. And if she lets him live, she's choosing a future filled with uncertainty and potential heartache.

But as she looks at Logan, his imperfections making him more endearing with every passing second, Laura feels a strange sense of peace. He's not the picture-perfect boyfriend she'd wished for, but he's something even better—he's real. With every stumble, every awkward silence, every shared laugh, he's proven that he has a life of his own, a heart that beats outside of her wishes.

The weight of her decision feels like a boulder on her chest. She thinks back to the fortune teller's words, the genie's warnings, and Rachel's skepticism. They all pointed to the same conclusion: love isn't something you can order from a cosmic menu. It's messy, it's complicated, and it's full of surprises.

But as she watches Logan, now more flawed than ever, Laura can't ignore the way her heart swells with affection. His stumbles and mistakes are endearing, a stark contrast to the flawless facade she'd once adored. The realization hits her like a ton of bricks: she's falling for him, not the idealized version she'd conjured up but the real, imperfect person he's become.

This revelation doesn't come without its share of turmoil, though. Laura's mind is a whirlwind of confusion and guilt as she thinks of Jake. She can't shake the feeling that she's betraying him by caring for Logan, that her love for him is a lie because of the magic that brought him to life. But every time she sees the raw emotion in Logan's eyes, the way he looks at her with hope and fear, she can't help but feel a deep connection.

The genie, watching the unfolding drama from the sidelines, shakes its head. "You're playing with fire, Laura," it warns her.

THE PERFECTLY IMPERFECT BOYFRIEND

But Laura can't help the way she feels. With every passing day, Logan's imperfections make him more human, more lovable. His awkwardness becomes endearing, his flaws a testament to his authenticity. Meanwhile, Jake's gentle concern and unwavering friendship remind her of the comfort she's always found in his presence. She's torn between the two of them, unsure of where her heart truly lies.

Chapter 12:

One rainy afternoon, Laura finds herself in the school's empty art room, her canvas a mess of colors and emotions. She's lost in thought, her brush strokes erratic and unplanned. Jake walks in, his footsteps echoing in the quiet space, and he stops, watching her for a moment before clearing his throat. "Hey," he says, his voice tentative. Laura looks up, her eyes meeting his, and she sees the love in his gaze—a love that's always been there, steady and true.

"Hey," she replies, setting her brush down. "What's up?"

Jake shuffles his feet, his eyes lingering on the canvas before meeting hers. "I just wanted to talk," he says. "I know things have been... weird."

Laura nods, her heart racing. "Yeah," she says, her voice small. "They have."

Jake takes a deep breath. "Look," he says, his eyes searching hers. "I know you're confused, but I just want you to know that I'm here for you. No matter what happens with... with all of this."

Laura looks away, the paint on her canvas blurring before her eyes. She feels a knot in her stomach, her feelings for both boys tugging at her in opposite directions. "I don't know what to do," she whispers. "I never meant for it to be like this."

THE PERFECTLY IMPERFECT BOYFRIEND

Jake steps closer, his hand reaching out to hers. "You don't have to choose," he says gently. "Not yet. Just... just let things unfold."

Laura nods, her eyes brimming with unshed tears. She's never felt so torn, so conflicted. Logan, with his newfound imperfections, is growing on her in a way that's both terrifying and exhilarating. And Jake, her rock, her confidant, her best friend—his love for her is as real and solid as the canvas beneath her trembling fingers.

The rain patters against the window, mirroring the tumult in Laura's heart. She pulls her hand away from Jake's and wipes her palms on her paint-splattered jeans. "I can't just ignore it," she says, her voice tight. "What I'm feeling for Logan... it's real. And I can't ignore what I feel for you, either."

Jake nods, his expression pained. "I know," he says, his thumb brushing over her knuckles. "It's just... I don't want to lose you."

Laura looks down at their intertwined hands, feeling the weight of her decision. She takes a deep breath and squeezes his hand in return. "You won't," she promises, her voice barely a whisper. "No matter what happens."

The days turn into weeks, and Laura finds herself torn between her two realities. With Logan, she experiences a love that's new, exciting, and a bit unpredictable. He surprises her with his quirks and imperfections, making her laugh when she least expects it. Their relationship feels like a rollercoaster of emotions, a thrilling ride that leaves her breathless.

With Jake, it's different. His love is like a warm blanket on a cold winter's night—comforting, familiar, and reliable. He's her rock, her confidant, the one person she's always been able to turn to. She cherishes their friendship and the possibility of more, but it's complicated by her burgeoning feelings for Logan.

The tension builds as Laura juggles her time between the two boys, trying to figure out her heart's true desire. Rachel, noticing the change in Laura, pulls her aside. "What's going on with you and Jake?" she asks, her eyes searching Laura's. Laura sighs, feeling the weight of her secret. "It's not just Jake," she admits, her voice low. "It's... it's complicated." Rachel nods, her expression understanding. "I know about the genie," she says. Laura's eyes widen in surprise. Rachel shrugs. "It's not rocket science, Laura. You've got a perfect boyfriend who appeared out of nowhere and a best friend who's been in love with you forever. The math isn't that hard." Laura looks at Rachel, torn between anger and relief. "How could you know?" Rachel gives her a sad smile. "Because I've seen it before," she says. "And it never ends well."

The words hang in the air like a storm cloud, darkening Laura's mood. She thinks about her mother's love for her father, a love that had been tested by hardship and imperfections, but had grown stronger with time. Could she have that with Logan? Or was it just a fairy tale doomed to unravel? And what about Jake, who had been there for her through everything? Could she ignore the love that had been there all along?

With trembling hands, Laura reaches for the lamp once more. She's lost, desperate for an answer that will end her confusion. She rubs it, and with a dramatic puff of smoke, the genie reappears. "What is your third and final wish?" it demands, its voice a thunderclap.

Laura swallows hard, the words sticking in her throat. "I wish to know who I truly love," she whispers. The room goes still, the only sound the ticking of the clock on the wall.

The genie's eyes flash with anger, and it points a finger at her. "You dare?" it thunders. Laura takes a step back, her heart racing. "You have made your wishes with haste and little thought for the consequences. Love is not a treasure to be found with a mere incantation!"

"Please," Laura begs, her voice shaking. "I didn't mean to—"

The genie's eyes blaze with fury. "You think love can be conjured and controlled?" it sneers. "You think your whims are more important than the fabric of existence?"

Laura's knees tremble as she stares at the angry creature before her. "I'm sorry," she whispers, feeling smaller than ever. "I didn't know."

The genie's expression softens a fraction. "You cannot force love," it says, its voice still stern but less thunderous. "You must choose with your heart, not your desperation."

Laura's eyes fill with tears. "I'm sorry," she whispers.

Chapter 13:

The genie's expression shifts, becoming less furious and more contemplative. "You have one final opportunity," it says, its voice softer now. "But remember, the choice must come from your heart. You cannot wish for love or for someone to love you. You can only wish for the clarity to see what is already there."

Laura's eyes widen with hope. "What do I do?" she asks, her voice shaking.

The genie looks at her, its eyes flickering with a mix of pity and frustration. "You must go to the place where you first wished for the perfect boyfriend," it instructs. "There, you will find a mirror. Look into it, and speak the name of the one you truly love. But beware, for the mirror shows not just your desires, but the truth of your heart."

Laura nods, her heart racing as she rushes out of the house, the words echoing in her mind. The wind whips her hair as she runs to the garage sale where she'd found the lamp. The rain has stopped, leaving the air crisp and clean. She spots the mirror, a simple oval frame with peeling gold paint, standing amidst the remnants of forgotten knick-knacks.

Her heart in her throat, Laura approaches the mirror. She looks into her own eyes, searching for the answer she so desperately needs. Her reflection is blurry, like her emotions, but she sees the truth in them. She's not looking for someone to complete her or to live up to an impossible ideal. She's looking for someone who loves her for who she is, imperfections included.

With a deep breath, she whispers, "I choose Jake." The mirror doesn't shimmer or crack. No grand magic happens. But in Laura's heart, something shifts. The confusion clears like fog lifting from a mountain top. The love she's felt for him for so long is still there, steady and strong.

The genie's voice, now gentle, fills her ears. "Your choice has been made. Now you must live with the consequences." Laura nods, feeling a strange mix of relief and dread. The genie vanishes, leaving her alone with her reflection.

Her heart racing, Laura runs back to Jake's house, the lamp tucked under her arm. She finds him in his room, surrounded by his beloved comic books, a look of concern etched on his face. "What's wrong?" he asks, noticing her disheveled state.

"I have to tell you something," Laura says, panting slightly. She sets the lamp on the floor and takes Jake's hand, her eyes searching his. "I made a mistake. I wish I could take it all back, but I can't. But I know now, I know who I truly love."

Jake looks at her, his eyes filled with a mix of hope and fear. "Who?" he whispers, his voice barely audible.

Laura takes a deep breath and meets his gaze. "It's you," she says, her voice firm. "It's always been you."

Jake's eyes widen in shock, and then a smile spreads across his face, lighting up his features. He pulls her into a tight hug, and she feels the warmth of his embrace seep into her bones. For the first time in weeks, she feels grounded, like she's made the right choice.

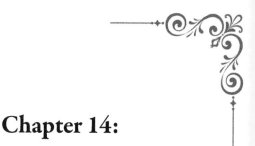

Chapter 14:

The moment, however is bittersweet. Laura knows that she must tell Logan the truth. She finds him in the park, sitting on the bench where they had their first date. His perfect exterior is a stark contrast to the tumultuous emotions roiling inside her. "Logan," she says, her voice shaking. "We need to talk."

He looks up at her, his eyes hopeful, and she can't help but feel a pang of guilt. "What's wrong?" he asks, his smile fading as he sees her face.

Laura takes a deep breath, her hand tightening around the lamp. "I... I have to tell you something," she says, her voice trembling. "I know I said I didn't know what to do, but I figured it out."

Logan's eyes light up, hope sparking within them. "You did?" he asks, his voice a mix of excitement and fear. Laura nods, her eyes brimming with tears. "I went back to the garage sale," she says, her voice barely above a whisper. "The genie said I could make one more wish. But it's not to erase you or change you. It's to choose who I truly love."

His expression falls, and Laura's heart breaks a little more. "And?" he prompts, his voice tight. Laura takes a deep breath, her eyes never leaving his. "I chose Jake," she says. "I love him."

The silence that follows is deafening. Rain starts to fall again, droplets pattering on the leaves of the trees above them, mimicking the rhythm of Laura's racing heart. Logan's eyes widen, and for a moment, Laura expects anger, or worse, despair. But instead, she sees understanding. He nods, his perfect features contorted with sadness. "I knew it," he says, his voice cracking. "I felt it, every time you looked at me differently."

"I'm sorry," Laura whispers, her voice breaking. "I never wanted to hurt you."

Logan looks down at his hands, which are now trembling. "I know," he says, his voice a mere echo of his usual confidence. "It's just..." He trails off, his eyes shimmering with unshed tears. Laura's heart feels like it's being squeezed in a vice. She never wanted him to feel pain, not when she'd created him to be her perfect escape.

But there's a spark in his eyes now, something she hadn't seen before. He stands up, brushing off his impeccable clothes. "I think I've always known," he says, his voice gaining strength. "But I had to try, didn't I? To be more than a fantasy." Laura nods, her eyes never leaving his. "You are," she says softly. "More than I ever imagined."

Logan smiles, a genuine smile that makes her heart ache. "Thank you," he says. "For giving me a chance to be more than just a figment of your imagination."

Laura nods, tears slipping down her cheeks. "What will you do?" she asks, her voice trembling.

Logan shrugs, a hint of a smile playing on his lips. "I don't know," he admits. "But I'm free now. And I'm going to enjoy it."

With that, he turns and strides away from Laura, the rain soaking him through, leaving a trail of wet footprints in the sand. Laura watches him go, feeling a strange mix of sorrow and admiration. He's right, she thinks. He's more than a wish come true—he's a person now, with a life to live.

Chapter 15:

In the months that follow, Laura sees glimpses of Logan around town. He's embraced his newfound humanity, stumbling through highschool, jobs, hobbies and the crazy world of dating, trying to find his place in the world. Each time she spots him, her heart aches a little less. He's happy, or at least he's trying to be, and that's all she ever wanted for him.

Meanwhile, Laura and Jake navigate the choppy waters of their new relationship. It's not the fairy tale she'd once dreamed of, but it's something better—it's real. They argue over what to watch on Netflix, bicker about who forgot to take out the trash, and laugh until their stomachs hurt over inside jokes that no one else understands. Laura learns that true love isn't about perfection, but about finding someone who makes your imperfections feel like quirks that make you uniquely you.

Jake, for his part, is patient with Laura's moments of doubt and guilt. He holds her when she cries about the weight of her decision, reassuring her that she made the right choice. He shows her that love isn't about being flawless, but about cherishing each other's flaws. And Laura, in turn, shows Jake the love he's been craving for so long. Their bond deepens with every shared secret, every tender kiss, every whispered 'I love you' in the dark.

Logan, on the other hand, takes his newfound freedom in stride. He discovers a love for cooking, much to the surprise of everyone who knew him as the boyfriend who could never burn toast. He opens a food truck, serving the town the most bizarrely delicious concoctions they've ever tasted. His charm and good looks still draw a crowd, but it's his endearing clumsiness that keeps them coming back. His journey to find himself is a hilarious, often embarrassing, and deeply human adventure that Laura and Jake can't help but follow from afar.

As the seasons change and the leaves turn gold, Laura and Jake sit on the same bench in the park where she'd once wished for a perfect boyfriend. They watch Logan's food truck bustle with customers, laughter spilling out onto the sidewalk. Rachel, now fully aware of the genie's influence, joins them, a knowing smile on her lips. "You guys okay?" she asks, nudging Laura with her elbow. Laura nods, leaning into Jake's shoulder. "Yeah," she says, a warmth spreading through her. "We are."

Jake wraps an arm around her, his eyes on Logan. "It's weird, isn't it?" he says, his voice thoughtful. "Seeing him like that?" Laura looks up at him, her eyes shining with unshed tears. "A little," she admits. "But I'm happy for him."

The genie's disappearance had left a peculiar aftertaste. Laura had felt a strange sense of loss when the creature had vanished, as if she'd been abandoned in the middle of her own love story. But she knew that the genie had given her the ultimate gift—the freedom to choose and the lesson that love wasn't about control or perfection. It was about growth and understanding.

Chapter 16:

Logan, now a fully realized human with a mind and soul of his own, faced the world with a mix of excitement and trepidation. The food truck was his new canvas, a place where he could express himself without the constraints of being the 'perfect boyfriend'. Each day brought new challenges and new tastes, but he relished the chance to be his own person, to make a name for himself beyond Laura's whims.

As the days passed, Laura watched from afar as Logan's life grew fuller and richer. His food truck, "The Wishful Plate," became the talk of the town. His signature dish, "Imperfectly Perfect Pizza," was a hit with teens and adults alike—a pie topped with the most unexpected ingredients that somehow harmonized into a delicious whole. It was a metaphor for his newfound existence, a celebration of imperfection.

One evening, as the setting sun painted the sky in hues of pink and gold, Laura found the courage to approach Logan's truck. The line of hungry customers stretched down the block, and she couldn't help but feel a twinge of pride.

"Hey," she called out, her voice barely audible over the sizzle of the pizza oven and the chatter of the crowd. Logan looked up, his eyes lighting up with recognition. He wiped his hands on his apron and made his way over, his smile a little less perfect, a little more genuine.

"Laura," he said, his voice warm. "What brings you here?"

She shuffled her feet, feeling suddenly shy. "I... I wanted to see how you're doing," she replied. "Your food truck is amazing."

Logan's smile grew a little sad. "Thanks," he said, his eyes scanning the line of customers. "It's been an adventure."

Laura nodded, watching him interact with the townsfolk. His charm was still there, but it was different—less forced, more authentic. He had a way with people that made them feel seen, heard, and appreciated—qualities she hadn't noticed before. "You're really happy," she said, her voice tentative.

Logan's gaze met hers, his expression earnest. "I am," he said. "It's weird, you know? Being real. But it's... good." Laura felt a pang of regret, but it was overshadowed by the happiness radiating from Logan. She'd given him a life, and it was clear he was making the most of it.

At school, Rachel watched Laura with a knowing smile. Laura felt her cheeks heat up under Rachel's scrutiny but said nothing. Rachel had been strangely supportive of Laura's decision, often remarking that she'd known all along that Laura's heart belonged to Jake. Laura couldn't help but wonder if Rachel had seen something in Logan that she hadn't.

Logan, for his part, had found a new spark in Rachel's company. Her sharp wit and sassiness were a refreshing change from the idealized version of himself that Laura had once created. Rachel didn't need him to be perfect; she liked him just the way he was. Laura noticed the way Rachel would sneak glances at Logan during lunch, the way her eyes lit up when he told a joke or shared a story about his food truck adventures.

One afternoon, Laura caught them in a quiet corner of the library, their heads bent over a book. Rachel looked up, her eyes meeting Laura's. "Hey," she said, her voice casual. Laura felt a twinge of something she couldn't quite name—not jealousy, but a sense of loss. Rachel had always been her confidant, the one person who knew her secrets. Now, Rachel had secrets of her own.

Logan looked up, his smile tentative. Rachel's eyes held something—a spark of interest, of connection. Rachel had always been the one to call out Laura's fantasies, to keep her grounded in reality. And now, she was falling for a boy who'd started out as one of those very fantasies.

The next few weeks passed in a blur of schoolwork and stolen glances. Laura watched as Rachel and Logan grew closer, sharing inside jokes and whispered secrets. Rachel, who'd once been so skeptical, now looked at Logan with a softness Laura had never seen before.

Chapter 17:

One crisp fall afternoon, Laura spotted them in the school's courtyard, surrounded by a riot of color from the changing leaves. Rachel's laughter was like a melody in the cool air, her eyes sparkling with mischief as she poked fun at Logan's latest culinary disaster. Logan took it in stride, his own eyes filled with affection and amusement. He leaned closer, his hand brushing Rachel's arm, and Laura's heart skipped a beat.

"Rachel," he began, his voice earnest. Laura held her breath, watching from the sidelines. Rachel's teasing smile faltered, her gaze locking onto Logan's. "I know this might sound crazy, considering..." He paused, looking down at his hands. "But I've never felt like this before. I mean, I know I've felt love before, but it was... different." Rachel's eyes searched his, looking for the truth behind the words. "It was perfect," he admitted, "but it wasn't real."

"What do you mean?" Rachel's voice was softer now, curiosity piqued.

Logan took a deep breath, his hand still hovering near hers. "I mean, Rachel," he said, looking up at her with those piercing eyes that had once been crafted by Laura's desires. "Would you like to go out with me? Like, for real?"

Rachel's mouth dropped open, a smirk playing on her lips. "Are you asking me out, Mr. Wishful Plate?"

Logan chuckled, his cheeks flushing a charming shade of pink. "I guess I am," he said, his voice a little shaky. "I mean, if you want to."

Rachel's smirk grew into a full-fledged smile. "Yeah," she said, her voice a little breathy. "Yeah, I'd like that."

Logan's hand closed around hers, his thumb tracing small circles on her skin. Laura felt a twinge of something—happiness, relief, perhaps a touch of nostalgia—but it was Rachel's reaction that captured her attention. Rachel's eyes lit up like fireworks on the Fourth of July, her laughter pealing through the courtyard.

"Now that you've asked me out," Rachel said, teasingly, "Let's see if reality can live up to your former perfection."

Logan rolled his eyes, a gesture Laura knew all too well. It was a quirk she hadn't noticed before, but now it was one of the things she found most endearing about him. "Reality's got nothing on me," he quipped, his eyes sparkling with a mischief that Rachel matched with her own. Rachel leaned closer, her smile growing wider. "Is that so?"

The air between them grew thick with anticipation, and Laura felt like she was intruding on a moment she wasn't meant to see. Rachel looked up at Logan, her eyes searching his. "Well, then," she said, her voice a playful challenge. "Prove it."

And before Laura could even blink, Logan leaned in and kissed Rachel. It was a kiss that held the promise of a thousand more—sweet and tentative, yet filled with the intensity of a first love. Rachel's eyes fluttered shut, and Laura could almost see the walls she'd built around herself crumbling away.

"Well, that was unexpected," Rachel murmured when they broke apart, her cheeks a rosy shade of pink.

Logan chuckled, his own face flushed with a mix of nerves and excitement. "Yeah, it was," he agreed, his thumb still caressing Rachel's hand. "But in a good way, right?"

Rachel's eyes searched his, a soft smile playing on her lips. "Yeah," she said, her voice barely above a whisper. "In a really good way." Laura felt a strange sense of peace wash over her as she watched the scene unfold. Logan was happy. Rachel was happy. And she, with Jake, had found something real. Maybe, just maybe, the genie's magic had worked out for everyone after all.

As logan thinks about his new life, he finds that the challenges of being human are not as daunting as he had once thought. His food truck, a symbol of his newfound independence, becomes a place where he can truly be himself. He takes pride in the way his customers light up when they taste his unique creations, and the way Rachel laughs at his kitchen mishaps feels more genuine than any laughter he had ever received from Laura. Maybe being human wasn't so hard after all.

Chapter 18:

As logan thinks about his new life, he finds that the challenges of being human are not as daunting as he had once thought. His food truck, a symbol of his newfound independence, becomes a place where he can truly be himself. He takes pride in the way his customers light up when they taste his unique creations, and the way Rachel laughs at his kitchen mishaps feels more genuine than any laughter he had ever received from Laura. Maybe being human wasn't so hard after all.

Logan starts to realize that he's developing a taste for the small, imperfect moments in life. The way Rachel's hair falls into her eyes when she's deep in thought, the way she bites her lip when she's nervous—these little imperfections make her beautiful to him. And as they spend more time together, he sees that Rachel appreciates his flaws, too. She doesn't expect him to be perfect; she just wants him to be himself.

He learns to navigate the choppy waters of human emotions with Rachel by his side. They share laughter and tears, frustrations and triumphs, each moment making their bond stronger. Rachel's skepticism has transformed into something softer, something that feels a lot like love. And with each passing day, Logan becomes more comfortable in his own skin, embracing the messiness that comes with being human.

He starts to enjoy the little imperfections that make life interesting—the way Rachel's penchant for spicy food sometimes leads to her sniffling and reaching for a napkin, the way her socks never match, and how she can never decide on just one movie to watch. These quirks that once seemed so alien to him now feel like home.

Logan throws himself into his new life with Rachel, learning to navigate the unpredictability of human relationships. He discovers the joy of holding her hand when she's upset, the comfort of her shoulder to lean on when he's feeling lost. Rachel's sharp wit and unfiltered honesty challenge him, pushing him to become the best version of himself. He stumbles, he makes mistakes, but with Rachel, he feels like he can face anything.

He starts to see beauty in his imperfections, the way a cracked teacup might still hold the perfect cup of tea. His clumsy attempts at cooking, once a source of embarrassment, become endearing to Rachel, who laughs as they order takeout yet again. He finds pride in his flaws, knowing they make him real.

One evening, as Rachel watches him with a mix of amusement and affection while he fumbles with a recipe, Logan catches her gaze in the kitchen's reflection. He sets down the spatula, his hands covered in batter, and wipes a smudge of flour from her nose. Rachel giggles, and Logan feels something shift within him—a warmth that fills the void left by the genie's departure. He's learning that love is not about being perfect for someone, but about being perfect for each other, flaws and all.

"You know," Rachel says, her eyes twinkling, "I think I might prefer your burnt cookies to those perfect ones you used to make."

Logan laughs, his hand shaking slightly as he pours batter onto the baking sheet. "Thanks," he says, a blush rising to his cheeks. Rachel's words stick with him, resonating in a way that Laura's adoration never had. With Rachel, his imperfections weren't flaws to be corrected; they were endearing qualities that made him unique.

He glances over his shoulder at Rachel, who's setting the table with a mischievous smile. She's the one who's taught him the joy of messing up, of trying new things even if they don't always turn out perfectly. Rachel's love for him is a wild, untamed force that accepts and cherishes his imperfections. It's a love that's grown from friendship, from shared laughter and heartaches. It's the kind of love that feels like home.

The timer on the oven dings, jolting Logan back to reality. He opens the oven door, half-expecting a cloud of smoke to billow out, but to his surprise, the cookies look edible. Rachel peers over his shoulder, her eyes lighting up with excitement. "They're not burnt!" she exclaims.

Logan laughs, feeling a thrill of accomplishment. "Maybe I'm getting better," he says, sliding the tray onto the cooling rack. Rachel snatches one up, breaking it in half and handing him a piece. "Here," she says, grinning. "A taste of your victory."

The cookie is chewy, with just the right amount of sweetness. It's not perfect, but it's perfect for them.

As Rachel's hand brushes against his, Logan feels a spark of excitement for what the future might bring. He's no longer bound by the constraints of his creation; he's free to experience the highs and lows, the joys and heartaches that come with being human. Rachel's laughter is the sweetest sound he's ever heard, her love a treasure more precious than any jewel he could have ever wished for. He looks at her, her eyes shining with mirth, and knows that he's found something real, something that can't be bottled or controlled.

Don't miss out!

Visit the website below and you can sign up to receive emails whenever Art Vulcan publishes a new book. There's no charge and no obligation.

https://books2read.com/r/B-A-MJTMC-CCRBF

BOOKS 2 READ

Connecting independent readers to independent writers.

Milton Keynes UK
Ingram Content Group UK Ltd.
UKHW040255181024
449757UK00001B/32